Okie-Dokie, Artichokie!
Grace Lin
VIKING

Marklee lived behind door 4B. From his window he could see treetops, stores, and a moving van. The moving van made Marklee especially happy, because that meant he was getting a new neighbor.

Mercer's Shop
SAFARI MOVERS
ROSES $5.00

"Hello, neighbor!" Marklee cried out as he jumped in front of the boxes and crates. "My name's Marklee! What's your name? Which apartment are you moving into?"

"My name is Artichoke," the giraffe said, slightly stiffly. "I'm moving into apartment 3B."

"3B," Marklee exclaimed. "Great, that's right below me!"

"Indeed," Artichoke said.

"Hey, if I get too loud or something, you can just bang on the ceiling and let me know," Marklee said. "I'll be real quiet for you."

"Thank you," Artichoke said, turning away with his boxes.

"Okie-dokie, Artichokie," Marklee said. "Nice meeting you!" And Marklee hopped on his way.

AFARI
MOVE
3B
3B
3B
3B
3B

MONKEY
ring
ring

The next morning, Marklee's alarm clock went off. "I hate waking up," Marklee thought as he put his pillow over his head.

Then ***BANG! BANG!*** came two thumps from the floor.

"The alarm must be bothering Artichoke," Marklee thought as he turned it off. "Sensitive fellow."

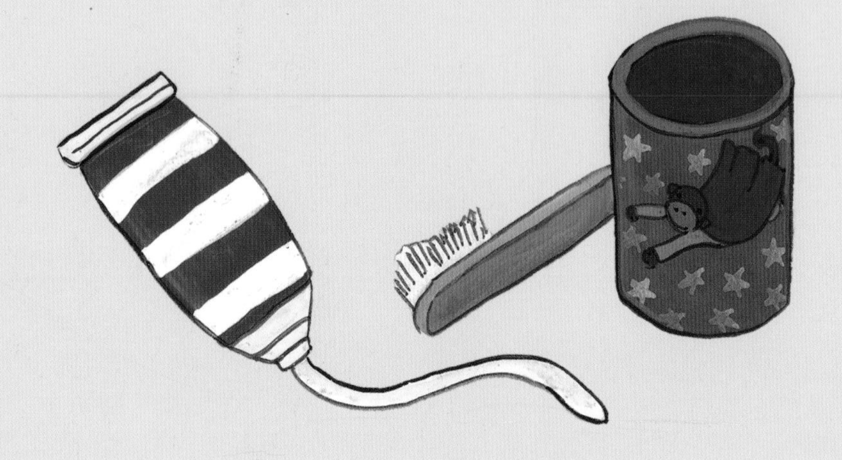

Marklee showered and brushed his teeth. While he was blow-drying his hair, he heard ***BANG! BANG!*** from the floor again.

"Gee, he's very sensitive," Marklee thought as he turned off his hair dryer.

BANG!
BANG!

All day long, Marklee heard ***BANG! BANG!*** from the floor.

When he fried his bananas.

When he did his morning exercises.

When he watched TV.

When he talked on the phone.

Super Monkey
BANG!
BANG!

Every day, Marklee walked on his tiptoes and spoke in whispers, but he still heard ***BANG! BANG!***

"That old Artichoke," Marklee thought, "he never gives a fellow a break."

One day, after a loud banging while Marklee was popping popcorn, Marklee decided that he had better talk to Artichoke. He went downstairs and knocked on the door.

No one answered.

"Artichoke," Marklee called loudly, "it's Marklee, your neighbor upstairs. You just banged on my floor. . . . I'd really like to talk to you."

Still no one came to the door.

"How rude!" Marklee said to himself when he finally left. "He could have at least opened the door! What an old grump!"

KNOCK!
KNOCK!

After that, whenever Marklee saw Artichoke, he walked right past him without saying a word. "If he doesn't want to talk to me, I don't want to talk to him," Marklee thought.

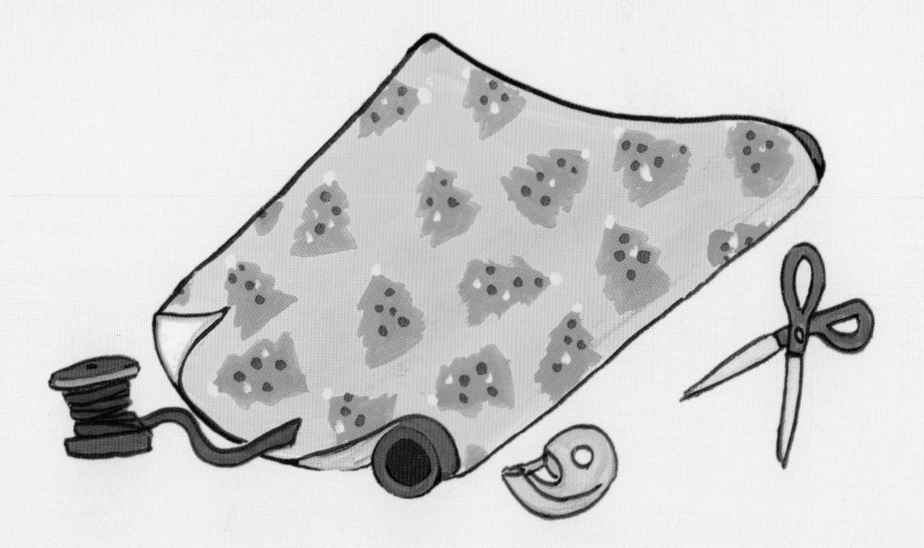

Winter came, and that meant Christmas. Marklee made snow monkeys and exchanged gifts with everyone. Everyone except Artichoke, that is.

"I don't want to give anything to that old meany," Marklee thought.

BANG!
BANG!

But one day Marklee received a large package. It was marked "To Artichoke Tall, Apartment 3B."

"Oops," Marklee thought. "The post office made a mistake."

BANG! BANG! came the noise from below.

Marklee stuck his tongue out at the floor. "Horrible old Artichoke! I should throw your package away!" And he put the package in the garbage bin.

But that night, as Marklee came home from a party, he saw Artichoke sitting by the window all alone.

"Maybe that was his only Christmas gift," Marklee thought, and he started to feel bad.

He went back to his apartment and got the package out of the garbage. "I guess everyone deserves a merry Christmas," Marklee thought, "even old grumps like Artichoke." Marklee, package in hand, went downstairs and knocked on Artichoke's door.

mousemas!
Peace

To:
Please wipe
our feet

This time, Artichoke opened the door.

"Hey, Artichoke," Marklee said. "The mail gave me your package by mistake."

"Oh!" Artichoke said, grabbing the box, "it must be my inflatable Velcro ceiling pillows! I've been waiting *so* long for them. Thank goodness they're here."

"They're what?" Marklee asked, puzzled.

"They're ceiling pillows," Artichoke said, "especially made for giraffes. Would you like to come and see what they're like?"

"Sure," Marklee said. "I'll help you set them up."

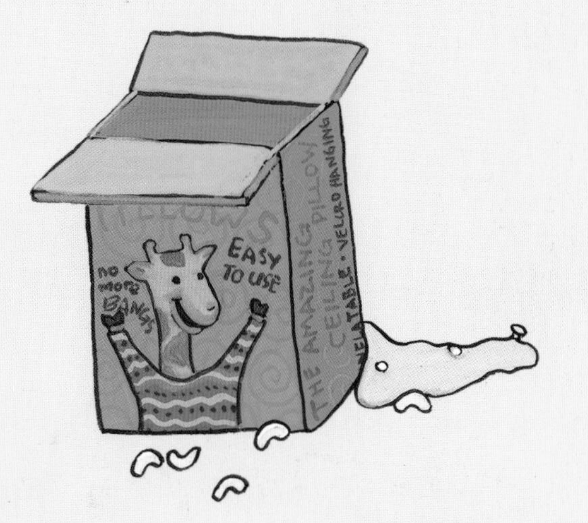

"I'm so glad they're here," Artichoke said as he lifted a pillow. "Now I can stop hitting my head on your floor."

"You've been hitting your head?" Marklee stopped blowing up a pillow and looked up. "I thought you'd been banging to keep me quiet."

"Oh no, really?" Artichoke said. "I was just thinking that you've been one of the quietest neighbors I've ever had. Would you like to stay and have a cup of cocoa?"

Marklee and Artichoke talked and laughed into the night. Marklee couldn't believe that this was the same Artichoke he had thought was so horrible.

"I'm glad you came over," Artichoke said. "I hope we'll be good friends now."

Marklee smiled. "Okie-dokie, Artichokie!"

To Ki-Ki, who says any book with a monkey in it is a good book

VIKING
Published by Penguin Group
Penguin Young Readers Group, 345 Hudson Street, New York, New York 10014, U.S.A.
Penguin Books Ltd, 80 Strand, London WC2R 0RL, England
Penguin Books Australia Ltd, 250 Camberwell Road, Camberwell, Victoria 3124, Australia
Penguin Books Canada Ltd, 10 Alcorn Avenue, Toronto, Ontario, Canada M4V 3B2
Penguin Books (N.Z.) Ltd, 182-190 Wairau Road, Auckland 10, New Zealand

First published in 2003 by Viking, a division of Penguin Young Readers Group.

1 3 5 7 9 10 8 6 4 2

LIBRARY OF CONGRESS CATALOGING-IN-PUBLICATION DATA
Lin, Grace.
Okie-dokie, Artichokie! / Grace Lin.
p. cm.
Summary: Each time Marklee gets a new neighbor he's excited to make a new friend, but the giraffe who just moved in downstairs seems to be a real grump.
ISBN 0-670-03623-4
[1. Neighborliness—Fiction. 2. Giraffe—Fiction.] I. Title.
PZ7.L644 Ok 2003 [E]—dc21 2002008294

Manufactured in China
Book design by Nancy Brennan